Emma's Eggs

To Stephanie,
Happy reading!
Margriet Ruurs.

By Margriet Ruurs
Illustrations by Barbara Spurll

Stoddart Kids

To Corrie and Marni, the world's best egg gatherers
— M.R.

To my Mom
— B.S.

Stoddart Publishing gratefully acknowledges the support of the Canada Council and the Ontario Arts Council in the development of writing and publishing in Canada.

First published in 1996 by Stoddart Publishing Co. Limited

Published in Canada in 1997 by Stoddart Kids,
a division of Stoddart Publishing Co. Limited
34 Lesmill Road
Toronto, Canada M3B 2T6
Tel (416) 445-3333 Fax (416) 445-5967
e-mail Customer.Service@ccmailgw.genpub.com

Published in the United States in 1997 by Stoddart Kids,
85 River Rock Drive, Suite 202
Buffalo, New York 14207
Toll free 1-800-805-1083
e-mail gdsinc@genpub.com

Canadian Cataloguing in Publication Data

Ruurs, Margriet, 1952 –
Emma's eggs

ISBN 0-7737-2972-0 (bound)
ISBN 0-7737-5898-4 (pbk.)

I. Spurll, Barbara. II. Title.

PS8585.U97E55 1996 jC813'.54 C96-930300-9
PZ7.R99Em 1996

Printed and bound in Hong Kong by
Book Art Inc. Toronto

Emma was changing. From a fluffy dandelion chick, she was turning into a feathery white hen.

Emma liked to step through the tall grass and scratch the ground for worms and seeds. She counted pebbles in the driveway and chucked around the house. Whenever she liked, Emma could go inside the chicken coop next to the barn.

Like the other chickens, Emma had made a cozy, shallow nest in the straw. Emma fitted on her nest like the lid on a cookie jar.

One day, when Emma was daydreaming, she had an irresistible urge to do something.

"Tok, tok, tok. . .TOK!" she said.

Emma hopped up and looked in the nest.
To her amazement, she had laid her first egg!
It was a bit small, perhaps, but it was perfect nonetheless.

That day, when the farmer's wife came, she saw Emma's egg. "Emma!" she said. "You laid an egg. Good girl!" She bent down, picked up Emma's egg and put it in her basket.

Emma was proud of her egg. She followed the farmer's wife to the house, hopped up on an empty apple crate, and peeked through the kitchen window.

The farmer's wife put a frying pan on top of the stove and cracked Emma's egg into the pan. She scrambled it with a fork.

"Tok!" said Emma. "Is *that* how they want my eggs? Then that's how I'll make them!"

So, when Emma laid another perfect egg the next day, she jumped on top of it and scrambled it with her feet.

"No, no, no, no, Emma!" cried the farmer, when he saw it. "That's *not* what you do with eggs!" And he shooed Emma away.

Emma followed the farmer when he took the other eggs into the kitchen. She hopped up onto the empty crate and peeked inside. She watched as the farmer dropped the eggs into a pot full of water.

"Tok!" said Emma. "Is *that* how they want my eggs? Then that's how I'll make them!"

The very next morning, Emma laid another perfect egg. Not in her cozy nest of straw, but in the chickens' water bowl.

"No, no, no, no, Emma!" cried the farmer's children, when they came to collect the eggs. "That's *not* what you do with eggs!" And they shooed Emma away from the water bowl.

Emma scratched her head. She was trying so hard to make perfect eggs, but nobody was pleased.

Emma hopped onto the crate below the kitchen window. At the table she saw the farmer, the farmer's wife and the farmer's children. They were doing something very strange. They were painting all of the eggs!

"Tok!" said Emma. "Is *that* how they want my eggs? Then that's how I'll make them!"

Emma laid two perfect eggs in the straw. She found a can of paint and a brush behind the barn. She was just putting on the finishing touches when the farmer's wife came to gather eggs.

"No, no, no, no, Emma!" she cried. "That's *not* what you do with eggs!" She shooed Emma away and threw out the paintbrush.

Very early the next morning, Emma watched as the farmer and the farmer's wife hid eggs all over the farmyard. They hid them behind shrubs and between daffodils. They even put one in the low branches of a tree.

"Tok!" said Emma. "Is *that* how they want my eggs? Then that's what I'll do!"

Over the next few days, Emma laid an egg in the feeding dish, and one behind a fence post, and another under the straw. She even left one beside the crate under the kitchen window.

"That's strange," said the farmer. "Emma has stopped laying." Then he spotted an egg behind the fence post and stepped on the one under the straw.

"No, no, no, no, Emma!" he cried. "That's *not* what you do with eggs!"

"Tok." said Emma.

That was it. That did it. If they didn't want her eggs, she wouldn't give them any!

Emma laid the next perfect egg in her cozy straw nest and she sat right on top of it. When anyone came near, she shooed them away. For days she sat on that nest like the lid on a cookie jar. Until one day, she had an irresistible urge to stretch. She hopped up, and looked at her egg. To her amazement, it started to crack. . .and creak. . . and wobble. . .and split.

Out of the shattered shell stepped a perfect dandelion chick.

"Tok," it said.

"TOK!!" said Emma.

"Yes, yes, yes, yes, Emma!" cried the farmer, the farmer's wife and the farmer's children. "*That* is what you do with eggs!"